PRINCESS Vinnea

AND THE

GULAVORES

INAUGURAL SERIES: STORY 2
OF THE
GUARDIAN PRINCESSES

This book was produced by the collective work of the Guardian Princess Alliance.

Written by Ashanti McMillon

Editorial Assistance:
Setsu Shigematsu
Ilse Ackerman
Kelsey Moore
Rié Collett
Ron Collett
Nausheen Sheikh

Illustrated by A. Das
Preliminary sketches by Mindy Vong
Wardrobe design by Kayla Madison

Cover and layout by Vikram Sangha

Common Core questions and activity by Tracy Hualde

Reading level assessment by Candice Herron

ISBN 978-0-9913194-0-4

Library of Congress Control Number: 2013957498

PRINCESS Vinnea AND THE GULAVORES

WRITTEN BY
ASHANTI MCMILLON
& THE GUARDIAN PRINCESS ALLIANCE

ILLUSTRATED BY A. DAS

ONCE UPON A TIME there was a princess named Vinnea. She lived in a land called Amani, a kingdom south of Primos. Princess Vinnea enjoyed spending her time in the village garden. She loved taking care of the plants and trees. After waking up each morning, she watered the garden and picked delicious fruits and vegetables. Princess Vinnea thanked the Earth for the food every day because it fed all the people of the kingdom. The garden produced the most beautiful fruits and vegetables because the plants enjoyed the way that she would sing to them:

I love the garden and the food it provides
From deep within the soil to the tallest, thickest vines
The fruits and vegetables are nature's gift
Our bodies they nourish and our spirits they lift
I plant the seeds and watch the garden grow
I take care of the plants that have sprouted in a row
I'm the princess of the garden, of the people, of the vine
I'll always protect what is yours and mine

The princess and the other farmers were excited for the Harvest Jubilee. This is the day when all the people of the kingdom come together to give thanks for the trees and plants and gather food from the garden. They all woke up early in the morning to start preparing for the celebration.

As they decorated the garden with colorful lanterns and streamers, a mysterious man driving a big red carriage passed through the village square. He did not stop or speak to anyone but instead rode on toward the king's castle.

Later that afternoon, while everyone was away from the garden, a thousand hungry caterpillars came and ate all of the fruits and vegetables. They ate and ate and ate! They devoured all of the fresh crops from the village garden all the way to the king's castle.

King Usambara was the ruler of Amani, and he also had a big garden filled with delicious fruits and vegetables. The king's gardener rushed into the court and screamed, "Your Majesty! All of the fruits and vegetables in the garden are gone!"

King Usambara exclaimed, "WHAT?! That was our entire supply of food! How can this be?!"

The gardener responded, "I don't know, sir. I don't know how this could have happened. What shall I do?"

Just then they heard a menacing voice from the doorway and saw the mysterious carriage driver. He said, "I know what you can do."

"Who are you? How did you get in here?" the king forcefully asked.

"Never fear, Your Majesty. I'm here to help you.
You're upset about your food, but I know what to do.
Your garden has a bad case of the Gulavores.
They eat and eat and still want more!
They're greedy caterpillars who eat everything in sight.
They will eat everything until the very last bite."

"How do you know this? Who are you? What is your name?" asked the king.

The mysterious man said in a sly tone,

    "My name is Danga and I come from the cold land of Gullon,

    where I make fruits and vegetables with my mighty wand.

    I'm a sorcerer who touches the soil of many lands.

    I create plants and food with my own two hands.

    I can bring plenty for each child, woman, and man.

    Lend me your ear, and I will tell you my plan."

Meanwhile, Princess Vinnea and the farmers returned to the garden to continue preparing for the Harvest Jubilee. As they entered the village garden, they saw that the crops were gone! All that remained were scraps of fruits and vegetables. Everyone was upset, and some children even began crying.

Princess Vinnea asked, "What happened to our garden? This was our only food supply."

Danga suddenly appeared from the crowd and said, "Don't worry, Princess. My name is Danga, and I come from the land of Gullon. I have enough food for all the people of the village. My food is very special and will make you feel satisfied."

Princess Vinnea asked, "What kind of food is this? Our people eat food only from the Earth."

Danga went to his carriage and pulled out an apple. The apple was the size of three regular apples.

"This is similar to the apple that is made from the ground,
but this one has been made bigger, shinier, and perfectly round.
I have enough for the whole village. Look at the huge potatoes,
giant strawberries, plump peaches, and enormous tomatoes.
I have pears the size of pigeons and gigantic grapes galore.
I have such an abundance! You'll be amazed by my store.
Give my food a try, it will make an amazing meal.
And don't worry, I'll give you an unbelievable deal.
My supply of food is endless! Come take what you need.
Take all that you want from my carriage and eat! Eat! EAT!"

At first, the people of the kingdom were very sad that all of their food was gone. However, after seeing the huge fruits and vegetables, they praised Danga and took food from his carriage. Princess Vinnea was not impressed. She was suspicious. Something did not seem right to her.

One of the farmers suggested, "Let's have the Harvest Jubilee in honor of Danga!" Everyone cheered in agreement except Princess Vinnea.

She thought to herself, *It is not natural for fruits and vegetables to be so big.* Rather than eat Danga's food, she decided to eat the leaves of the Brumie trees.

Sure enough, after the farmers ate Danga's food, they began to get sick, and terrible sores grew on their skin.

Worried about her people, Princess Vinnea
wrote a letter to her friend Princess Terra
and asked her to come right away.

When Princess Terra arrived, she and Princess Vinnea returned to the garden. They were sad to see it so empty. They planted seeds into the soil and together they said,

"What happened to our beautiful garden that we cherish?
Please grow back the fruits and vegetables, so our people won't perish.
We love how your food makes us healthy and strong.
Please return to normal. Help us prove Danga wrong."

Suddenly, a strange noise came from one of the bushes.

"Munch! Munch! Munch!"

Princess Terra looked closer and exclaimed, "Princess Vinnea, look at this caterpillar! This is a Gulavore. They eat everything in sight. They come from the land of Gullon."

Princess Vinnea said, "Gullon? That is where Danga comes from. I bet that he brought them here to destroy our gardens."

"But why?" Princess Terra asked.

Princess Vinnea replied, "I think that he wants us to buy his big fruits and vegetables. But something must be wrong with them because they make the people sick."

The two princesses found Danga's carriage. Inside, Princess Vinnea picked up a big red book titled *Magic Spells for Plants and Bugs*. As the princesses looked through the book, they found the magic spell that Danga used for making his unusual fruits and vegetables. The spell mixed magic with toxic chemicals.

Princess Vinnea said, "I know that there are good and helpful chemicals, but Danga's are harmful."

Princess Terra said, "His food is not made with love. What kind of person would make food that makes people sick?"

Princess Vinnea said, "We must stop the people from eating Danga's food!"

Princess Terra added, "Let's take his spell book, so he can't use it to do any more harm."

In the spell book they also found a page about the Gulavores. "Look, here is how to get rid of the Gulavores in the garden. All we have to do is sing this song."

Gula! Gula! Gula!
Bellies full of leaves
Gula! Gula! Gula!
Time to fly beyond the trees!

Even though the people were sick, they still wanted to celebrate the Harvest Jubilee. King Usambara came to the village square to honor Danga.

At the same moment, Princess Vinnea and Princess Terra arrived.
Princess Vinnea announced, "Do not eat the food that Danga gave you. His food is the reason you have all become so sick! He brought Gulavores from his homeland to attack our garden, so that he can sell us his dangerous food!"

"No, I'm here to help you," Danga said. "These fruits and vegetables make you feel full. They are good for you!"

Princess Vinnea said, "No, these fruits and vegetables are not good for the people! They're dangerous! Admit it, Danga. You ruined our garden in order to sell us this unhealthy food!"

Danga said, "I have nothing to admit."

"Princess Vinnea," King Usambara said as he walked toward her, "even if what you say is true, if we planted new seeds in the garden today, we will have to wait many months for the crops to grow."

"Don't worry. Just follow us to the village garden," Princess Vinnea said.

When they arrived, the Gulavores were everywhere! They were all over the garden. The princesses sang the magic spell together:

Gula! Gula! Gula!
Bellies full of leaves
Gula! Gula! Gula!
Time to fly beyond the trees!

All of a sudden, the Gulavores turned into beautiful, colorful butterflies. The garden was filled with a rainbow of butterflies.

The princesses continued singing:

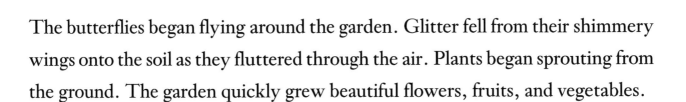

Gula! Gula! Gula!
Carrying sweetness like bees
Gula! Gula! Gula!
Time to fly beyond the trees!

The butterflies began flying around the garden. Glitter fell from their shimmery wings onto the soil as they fluttered through the air. Plants began sprouting from the ground. The garden quickly grew beautiful flowers, fruits, and vegetables.

Danga cried, "How can this be?"

Princess Vinnea replied, "We used your magic book to break your spell, Danga!"

"That's right!" Princess Terra added. "The Earth has helped the people once again. The wing dust of the butterflies fertilized the garden, and its magic made all the plants grow quickly!"

Danga screamed, "No! You have ruined my plans!" He started to run away toward the Brumie woods.

"Not so fast!" Princess Vinnea said. She opened up the spell book and sang:

Seeds and soil, you reap what you sow
Greed and spoil, fake food is what you grow
Leaves fallen from trees, dirt to mud
Turn the wicked Danga into a bug!

Danga was instantly transformed into a dung beetle. Princess Vinnea quickly scooped him up and dropped him into a jar. "Now, my little friend, you can no longer harm anyone." All the people cheered! The village garden began flourishing again and was more beautiful than ever.

Princess Vinnea announced, "Everyone, please enjoy the new fruits and vegetables that our garden has given us today." The villagers ran to the garden with great excitement. Everyone ate the fresh crops, and by eating the fresh fruit and vegetables, those who were sick from eating Danga's food were healed.

King Usambara thanked Princess Vinnea and Princess Terra for saving the village garden. He asked, "Would you restore my garden too? I would be forever grateful."

Princess Vinnea said, "We would love to, and now that the garden is restored, let's finally have our Harvest Jubilee!"

That day was the busiest and happiest Harvest Jubilee in the history of Amani. Princess Vinnea turned Danga's food into stones that the people used to decorate the garden. Everyone had a merry time. They ate and played music to celebrate the garden and the princesses' victory. They danced and sang this song to thank the Earth for providing an abundance of plentiful, healthy food as the sun set over the beautiful garden:

We pledge to do what is just and fair
To do our best to protect and care
For all living beings great and small have worth
We shall come together to take care of our Earth
Growing strong like a tree from healthy food
We will nurture the garden because it nourishes us too
We shall protect the seas, skies, and lands of all nations
To be cherished and shared by the next generations

The End